Entice 2

I0570840

BROKEN

&

EROTIC

THE BROKEN STORY

Andre Roberts and Friends

BROKEN & EROTIC

Printed in the United States of America

ISBN-13: 978-0692407332
ISBN-10: 0692407332

Printed by Createspace 2015
Published by BlaqRayn Publishing Plus 2015

Building An Empire In Ink

BROKEN

&

EROTIC

THE BROKEN STORY

Andre Roberts

BURNT

legs
in
the
air
swayed back
up to serve
the kiss
of bite ting lips
ready to devour
that glue upon
chew upon
to drive
the minted
the taste to stroke
Pull from this....This vision
not a chance
this fire has started!!!!
stolen of breath,
no words
in which
to speak
Burn!!!!!!
Can you hear
those sirens horn
wanting to
lose myself
inside
My body
is all
a
blazed
in heat
we find those
Heated passions

Entice 2

well engaged
lose myself
i chose to do
Just let go
Your lips
should be cold
to swirl this tongue
and be consumed
Burnt i say
as i lay
between
your thoughts
as i dig in
to show my best
wetted bliss
the flickers
twists and turns
inside the jiggers
the body churns
a body rush
beyond control
as i shudder
my lost for words
this sweat brakes
as i breed
a hunger quest
a drop to knees
and the shivers
with its shake
those blinking eyes
to quench the thoughts
spent I'm not
i am enthused
my body used
to gain your please
I spread to please
Flick to tease

Entice 2

Then a taste
No need for haste
time well taken
for this drink
in wines we taste
never in a waste
the heated prance
of new romance
cant defeat
our hours glance
BURNT IT IS !!!!!!
in this our flavor
and in its flame
a taste and tender
a selfless render
of passions throw
within this blender
But So you Know
this slice of spice
this wanted desire
this hearted inspire
by visions design
of friends admire
of lusts attire
that someone else's
love retired
amazing
what man throws away

AR/ALN

FEEL

SHE
sat by me
soften ,
moist
wet
as lips approach
skin of silk
tenderances
maidens twinge
tolerances
velvet breeze
as she prances
violet scent
in the romances
i savor a view
to just remember
to see
if
i
can
this voyage
so intricate
it flows me well
it takes me out
inside my shell
so so missed
within the kiss
as she shakes me
for my response
hardened moments
freeze my thoughts
a lip in lock
to bend my wave

Entice 2

touchings firm
i render hands
my Christmas gift
for i am lonely
with that her soothe
we lock in love
we twist ourselves
like as a swan
the quietness
of our body's
the song we mate
has its tune
a seasoned dance
as we crumble
the weakness of
the lust we bear
the sweat of heat
makes me wonder
how far we rose
to aim to please
at each time
we tossed this feeling
breaking backs
is that our flex
hammer blows
we tuned our body's
just to scream
and hear ourselves
as we lace
this
dance of prance
in its hunger
we don't retract
the new found high
is our Delmar
can we quench
this heated throw

Entice 2

with eyes closed
i do remember
it was the task
that made my traction
as i lay here
on my back
in of this
hospital room
DAM
SHE BROKE ME!!!!!!!!!
PAINED
AND
LOVING
IT
I WAS HUNGRY...

FIRST DATES

UNIQUE IN FORM

EMOTIONAL RISE

CREATES THE STORM

A VENDOR'S GAME

A SHOW AND TELL

AND SOMETIMES

DAM

A GIFT FROM HELL

WHAT'S IN THE LIE PT 5

AR/ALR/RD

Awesome and true
to so many ,
and true also
they might go wrong
,for true love should be given
every fight
to make
it right,
but so many things happen
in relationships

Entice 2

too plenty,
the pair
won't give and take
both ninnies,
they let it go dead,
the spark is not there,
lost in the head,
showing no care
for what can
you
do
when
it
happens
to
you

BUT WAIT!!!!!!!
I'VE GONE TO FAR
THIS IS A TIME
WHEN THEY FIRST MET
THE GET TO KNOW
AND WHAT THEY SAW

Early
in the afternoon
a box of candy
was delivered
flowers too
and a note
admirers fan
to stroke a blaze!!!!!
in this note
the words of praise
of hopes to see
the want to be
the string of things

one never sees
the claims of sight
past pleasant nights
a wishful tone

ET PHONE HOME
IF HE WAS THERE
THE THINGS HE'D SHARE
SEALED AND KISSED
THE HOW HE MISSED
IN ITS WISHING
A BEG YOU SEE
A WISH THAT HE
WANTS TO BE

Going back
a couple days
Chance meeting
fender bender
Scrolling thru
a text mess
he sent!!!!!
her
The
mistress
possible
next!!!!!
,
not paying attn.
Rolled thru
a stop sign
bashed and dented
she wondered how???
She saw something
in his eyes
Exchanges of info
and

Entice 2

AND
then
the surprise note !!!!!!!!

NOT REALLY CARING
BUT LONELY IN STATE
HMM A DATE
WONT BE LATE
AND THERE THE CHANCE
TO LEAVE HER HOME

so their hook up is next?
almost but not yet
still working on it
the thoughts that pass
like wine in a glass
sipped and savored
and then agree!!!!!!
shape still forming
this new idea
might be fun
this time of year

NIGHTS LIGHT

:AR

DREAMS
I WAKE UP FROM
SEEING MAYBE
OF PAST EVENTS
REAL EVENTS
WITHIN MY DOME
OR
COULD IT BE
THE FUTURE
OF THE THINGS
THAT I HAVE SEEN
SWINGING BLOWS
UPON THE NOSE
RELEVANT SHOWS
A SIGHT TO SEE

The walk upon
a lake of thoughts
upon such shores
to open doors
to trace a road
an avenue
the rear in signs
a look back view
deepened rifts
that run a drift
never solved
never resolved
until the morning
when all comes clear
i
look
upon

Entice 2

the
new
a different
muse
to start the day
or maybe not
depends what plays
i toss
different stones
collected scenes
reviewed by me
that different dance
the man with lance
my hero's plan
with land and grants
my woman's life
and how i fit
and how i conjure
to win this round
a daily quest
with shield in hand
for her to see
this better man
for her to cherish
and adore
for her to wish
for no one other
it is that deep
within this dream
creates the steam
as passions flow
creating paths
the new day holds
or
i wish
i missed
our loss of love

Entice 2

in hind and sight
mistakes that broke
a road taken
this is no joke
trust now lost
honesty
we are now foes
for all to see
the mend is not
why is this so
never spoken
don't you know
so we rent
a piece of heart
wanting never
to be apart
excuses makes
us TO relate
to tell this lie
of our mistakes
we
bend the truth
and make it fit
removing chances
of
our great split
and
so the fears
lend themselves
within this dream
OF MANY TEARS
to
make
us
think
and then become
new

Entice 2

friends
again
and our dislikes
and our cares
back burner hits
sitting in chairs
remember now!!!!!!!
its in my head
within this dream
that i create
it may not be
just and how
as i said it
it is for you
now to decide
WORK IT OUT
or
LET IT SLIDE!!!!!!! :AR

CLASS ACTION:SH/AR

Twin peaks
satin skin
rich chocolate
smoothness
DEVOURS HIM
She
you
erotica
picS sEZ
wow

.

Moon light *****
shining
on his skin ,
Richness
in every glistening shape
Light falls*****
on Showing him
in a beautiful
of the light.
Every bit
a trophy
to be had
at least
this night
Light shimmering!!!!
on her beauty
Showing him
her loveliness
He responds!!!!
to her softness

HMMS THE WORD
AS HIS MOUTH DROPS

Entice 2

he recomposes
She !!!!
this fine woman
In turn moves
a little closer
to view him better
and desire
his firm body !!!!
clearly displayed
as he moves slowly
closer and closer
in his moves!!!!
Her body betrays
her rising heat
as her heart beats
a little faster
the pains of passion
are now in touch
He smiles
as she approaches
his eyes !!!!
taking her in
visions of glass
seductions road
now in trance
as she moves
forward
in the shower!!!
in curtain
this pleasured dream
his mental view
brought forward
dances of the quest
thoughts bent over
to be un-sleeved
it leaves a shiver!!!
as he looks on

Entice 2

the mind is groping
fondle of plays
tenderly taste ting
her review
oh this her structure!!!
so devised
intertwined
body heat
like wines engulfment
the walking head buzz
that drunken bed mate
sHe smiles!!!
as he approaches
her eyes
taking him in
as she moves pass!!!
walking fast
reviewed the scene
gives the thought
cleared the entry
and grabs her lover:
SH/AR

I SEE YOU:AR

was what she saw
she chose to view
the me to see
as i did show
the glimmer
the shivers
the rivers
of the soul
as she
went deeply
into me
ya know that look
that one that stares
and sees past you
like your not there
its now i wondered
was i ok
a view to be killed
a view to be stilled
a taste to lavish
then replenish
how could i know
whats in her mind
did i
look
like someone else
a past retrenched
a fonder blunder
of covers under
a maybe wonder
a time that was
a missing man
her sisters
past lover

Entice 2

a missed romance
that sometimes along time ago lings
of missing ones chance
a banned romance forbidden
by some but an adventure
so entwined
so evolved
so refined
so in depth
and so inviting
a different sum
to this equation
i saw her
looking at me
for me to see
eyes sparked with lings
so devouring
so enticing
and she
saw me
wanting
to
know
first words never spoken
from across a room
muse as it were
filled with mums
feeling hmms
as we glance
the emotions
of dance
within our tune
within our sways
NOW
IF ONLY THE CHANCE:
AR

WITHIN THE NIGHT PT1

AR/BDSP/SH

PAST 12 AM
most Folks
have gone to bed
its the start
of many thoughts
evenings avenues
a road of the lone
not wanting to stay
home
a hunger
for those unknown
to open UP
the new day
a time for playing
kissings of JISTS
days new breathe
OF THE REATCHED
for some
hands upon
the new found friends
i think you know the rest
THE Hungry games
the games we
Players play
THAT game OF LUST
With Out THE shame
Just raw in fire
as in their veins
Like liquid GLASS
pulsing through
An apEX tight
the needs to feed
players grounds

Entice 2

weary hounds
lone some
hints
as the hungers
get to know
the want to see
the who's we meet
and in their games
do we retreat
SHE
stepped
into my life
a certain wife
of another
but here she stood
all in the hood
and banged
on my desire
and as she spoke
sez her
Indeed
my lust for fun
has brought me to this
way to many sleepless nights..
I'm like a animal
in heat..i shed
Not sure how
to end this hunger
and to this end
the insane ways
mind games plays
For the who
I really am
a lonely player
without a band
feeding off
the weak and lonely

Entice 2

to get to what
I really need
to feed upon
my empty soul..
i Once had
a great lover
but inner demons
chased him away..
Once had a great lover
but my inner demons
chased her away..
KARMA HAS
SUCH HUNGERED FRIENDS
A QUEST IN HAND
LUSTS RUN A MUCK
One step forward
and she IS gone
One step back
and she IS looking
FOR SOME ONE ELSE
No demons hiding
They come out
siding
PutTING them both
on the side line
Shafting them down
FOR SOMEONE ELSE
THIS QUEST IS BEST
BUT IN MY CRIES
I LONGED FOR HER
It starts with a thought
Not one that's taught
Just
fires
up
the old AND BOLD
Images not sold

Entice 2

Hold on
Got to
roll on
her
so as i listened
her words did say
He turned me on
like no other
damn these evil tricks
my mind
had to play ..
The devil has
some kind of control
over me I swear...
i am that bold
I search for
that love he brought
me out and about
searching for
the replacement him
and of the me
ill never find it..
Come on baby
help kill the demons
inside of me
back in the day..
i would play
and buy this game
and maybe stay
she lives
in my
every thoughts and dreams...
Damn you devil... Why me? :
BDSP/AR/SH

WITHIN THE NIGHT PT2

BDSP/AR/SH/MILDRED SEEGERS

As we ripen
having patience
is a wonderful
it saves a lot
of wear and tear
on the nerves
you know the rest
the untold
and folded
this story's best
and what persuaded
i continue
in this venue
an am want
on my desires
so here i listen
to her story
with my eyes forward
upon her breast
i licked my lips
upon this taste
to hear her gist's
whiles hesitate
i hear her speech
i see her glow
within her eyes
the want to know
in show she did
that beauty flinch
the rinse of grace
all in its shower
broken upon
in confess

Entice 2

so misused
by her mates
within that fury
vengeance rose
to where it is
as she tells
her bitter self
is on the shelf
as we prod
the self impose

that fury
to tender down
And receive
the warmth of a new
beginning trends
inside bends
all
in
its
fury
from
the
fury
wasn't long after
her he came looking
for his misses
and hers stories
he knew her wants
he knew her well
just by her eyes
oh he could tell
Her heart
her mind
The inner workings
of her tortured soul

Entice 2

The body that needs
to be touched
held and excited
by a passion

that is the she
always longed for
but never
has received
in her mind
wasn't long after
her he came looking
for his misses
and hers stories
he knew her wants
he knew her well
just by her eyes
oh he could tell
that is the she
always longed for
but never
has received
in her mind
As she sat there
not sure what
to tell her husband
she knew she had to
to seduce him
to get him to go
get his mind off
the situation
at hand
Mind working
on over load
gave   me
a little more time
to play this game

Entice 2

tension begins
to show its face
almost disgraced
within his actions
She knew
all the right places
to touch on him..
and soothe his mind
and so he left
and just to now
her story
needs a dressing
that's no matter
i heard the latter
wanting to prod
the self impose:
BDSP/AR/SH/MS

EXOTIC:AR

Any one different
from what you
have grown to know
forbidden by some
but
in her

she shows
oh she does know
the get to know
stepping on toes
as gentile flows
within her grace
away

fruit you say
no stay
and play
must get away
but in that is
the greatest
of lies

for she is a wonder
one not to flounder
as gorgeous goes
you dent relent
You'll pay that rent

she is your tastes
she does relate
she feels your praise
and sees your eyes
reads you well

Entice 2

makes your
heart swell
within the well
emotions tell
and in its speech
the now released
words you speak
without control
no mistake

as far
as cultures go
it is in her show
you'll learn and grow
and there

she will go
inside your head
you wont know
fantastic is
the breath you take
when you first meet
tis no mistake
different
her

a glow to show
the rose on top
the thorns of life
and in its kiss
lands the bliss
and see ur fears
placed on chairs
loss of gears
in the touch
in her walk
she wakens you

Entice 2

from the view
enticing
devising
the romance flows
within your thoughts
you have been dropped
because
she
Is

EXOTIC :AR

I BOW DOWN

AR/SH/ALR/DH

IT IS THIS GIFT
EMOTIONS BRING
IT IS A LIFT
THE HEART
DOES SING
IT IS IN PRESENTS
THE LIGHT
TO SEE
NOT OF BLINDERS
SOME FOLKS
DO BRING
OF HATREDS
BEST
SOME OF THEM!!!!
FEAR VENDORS
INVENTORS OF
JEALOUSY'S MYTH
CREATORS OF
THE UNREST
THE REST
LOST IN LIFE
LOOSE
IN THE WAY OF
STREETS
THE PARENT BODY!!!!
UNJUST FINGERS
IS THEIR ROMANCE
AS THEY POINT
AND SHOW THE YOU
OR IS IT?
A SEASONED BATCH
OF ILL FAY TEDDY STEW
JUST TO CONFUSE

Entice 2

REVERSE THE VIEWS
OF THIS FOGGY DANCE
BEAT DOWN MONGERS!!!!!
OH THEY HUNGER
TO BRING THE DOWN
IN TALENTS UP
IMAGINE
HARD TO FOCUS
IN THE RUSTY
TO JUSTIFY!!!!
THE WHY
THEY LIED
AND TRIED
PAST REASON
TO REPLY
IS IT NOT
INTERESTING AT BEST
THE TIME THEY TAKE
TO CREATE THIS STATE
ILLUSIONS !!!!

on painted tint
shady hits
upon the mists
a war!!!!
of spoken words

FIC-TICH-IOUS FRIENDS
INTO THEIR BENDS
WANTING THE END
OF PIECE
AND PLENTY
THEIR OWN

grown mistakes
no retakes
a glance

Entice 2

of fancy
i bow down !!!!!
for this i know
for in its show
ALL DOES GLOW
one does look:
AR/SH/DH/ALR

WHAT'S IN THE LIE pt1

A LOVE REVEALED/AR

Nerves fighting
the urge to walk,
desire
takes over
wanting to stay
by the spark
that reflected light
the swing of balance
emotions height
the story
so unyielding
twists and turns
sought after words
so revealing
her heart sank!!!!
as the story was told
heard before
from so many
but in her heart!!!!
she knew the truth
been here before
just last June
half an hour ago
it was his touch!!!!!
a fraggered dance
and in his hands
refined romance
so soft he spoke
it was his game
hopes to poke
so he
told this story
and in his mind!!!!

Entice 2

she will
take this toke
blowin
smoke
cause
she will hear
and give me some
i got this catch
i fished it well
his ego spoke
within his StRoke
ill spank that babe
rack that body
love till dawn
ohh so hEarty
she will buy
my game
even insane
i got this lane
ill drive my car
so he built
this great line
to run pass
his so divine
in his sight
in his review
this body fine
is mine to play
he saw her beauty
well defined
he saw the grace
of her fine lines
he saw her structure
he felt her taste
his dreams of rock
upon that waste
legs of length

Entice 2

breast of queens
mountains high
THE taste of wine!!!!
and in her
simmer
the quakes of shakes
she drops me like
a new born kid
in his thoughts
he rose

NEVER NOTICED
HER REVIEW pt 1:
A Love Revealed /AR

WHAT'S IN THE LIE PT2

A LOVE REVEALED/AR

And when he rose
the fire did swell
Burned like
she was standing
at the gates of hell
Passion so strong,
only known
by a few
His seasoned soul
Knew exactly
what to do
Kissed her firmly
on her lips
Hands moving slowly
over her hips
Finding that spot
between her thighs
HENCE THE LIES!!!!
Room filled
with erotic cries
Taken with
such sexual bliss
To be one
with his body
is to exist
OHH SO SHE FELT HIM !!!!
enjoyments best
for this he craved
was in his eyes
but this she knew
went with the lies
just to atone
her lies

Entice 2

her own
and when all done
the end of fun
she then decided
to tell her own
A Love Revealed/AR

Whats In The Lie PT3

A Love Revealed/AR

So two can play this game
If he could, then she the same
A man she had met once before
Thoughts she imagined behind closed doors
Tonight she was going to engage
Impurities fueled by rage
Off to a land of ecstasy
Not caring who would see
She gazed long into his eyes
Hesitation, surprised
Turned away and buried the cries
This night tainted by lies
Alone lost in the fog
He sensed something was wrong
Pushed her hair to the side of her neck
Kissed her gently as she wept
Laid her softly on the bed
Whispered tonight our desires will be wed
His tongue created a rhapsody
As it moved over her body
Lost in his beautiful song
Touch for which she had longed
No longer seeing straight
Letting go of all the weight
Lust ever so strong, forget the wrong
Entwined with him is where she belonged

A Love Revealed/AR

MY TEARS:AR

SHAKEN MOMENTS
my tears
cry their own
so tested
in emotions
fears dwelling
within the heart
to release
and grasp
the edgings
of visions
so moved
invented events
a hearts laments
in shares
of caring
i weep
internal
for seeing brings
contested views
i swell within
my convictions
and share pain
with every drop
as angry thoughts
convince emotions
dont
want
ever
mists
my tears hear
the seeing eye
as we destroy
ourselves in life

and human
i bend at thoughts
wars best friend
we never look
and see us well
the land we have
oh we must fight
and stand a ground
mens just and gist
incorrect evils
with a twist
to reinvent

JUST WHAT MEANS ALL
NOW WE HAVE GONE
AND OUR CHILDREN
GROW TO KNOW
THOSE MISTAKES
OF OUR FOLLIES
AND IN OUR LAKE
OF TEARS WE SHED
AND IN ITS CRIES
THE WARS MUST STOP
A CHILD HEARTS LOST
BY OUR DISAPPERS
THEY WILL HAVE THE TEARS
OF THEIR OWN
AND IN THOSE HEARTS
THEY'LL GROW TO KNOW :
AR

MORTAL THOUGHTS:AR/SH

I CAME HOME HUNGRY
wantin that thing
playin wit sex
and ear erect
thoughts of plenty
as u get older
u want more
but the body don't listen
the thoughts glisten
as you fantasize
Yeah ?. Really
How do you
overcome it.
jump up on it
try to
get it rubbed
more than mental
even dental
in a rental
of ur mind
got no choice
get it done
or get an xtra
for the fun
You have an appetite
On you like a hungry lion
that of a good meal
the taste is in the mouth
being too much
I jump
You need always
till u drop
and want sum more
or you may flop

Entice 2

What you want me to do
i am hungry
not for food only
I'm on a diet
can u just
feel it
rub it
touch it
mentally
grab it
flag it
tag it
wit ur body
wake it
shake it
taste it
make it scream
You want to hold me
I see you like
a taller tower
imma hold you
and massage you
rub you
and look on you
as a thing of beauty
let them get acquainted
Are you ready
is it wet yet
My flowing river
you making me crazy
Sex on my mind
You know it
starts to swell
the heat of
that tasty meat
that well cooked
in the heat

Entice 2

Your feeling freaky
By golly man
what have you done to me
rose u up
and began to scatter
You makes me hungry
You there
hitting that batter
began a flatter
and deepened pick
You woke me up
workin on it
that sleeping lion
better whip that thing
with its own desire
kinda that way now

ITS A STEW
A MEAL
SPICY
ALMOST DICEY
WITH THE RICE
YES I'M READY:
AR/SH

BEAT DOWN:AR

SURE
i did steal!!!
taken from
another lover
within her heart
i showed myself
i ran through it
and placed my TASTE
like Tchaikovskys 1812
the cannons rolled
will did tell
overtures in
the moods were
fast and quickened
smooth and serene
we rode a horse
to our extremes
sailed upon
our stream of fate
then the opening
and through the gates
i whipped upon
her mind and mine
we delved and dealt
our headed games
oh how it felt
we played and talked
as we sought
the finds of life
the things i brought
we trashed our vents
forever tight
swang that thing
as so we waltzed

Entice 2

and danced till dawn
the love we made
put me in traction
a spastic grind
we tend to do
a breath
taken
shakin
then shook
as
i
glide
and
grin
for eye
was happy
so softly
she stroked me
rose and toasted
hidden feelings
of this
my conquest
as she showed
her passions best
i had the yells
the needs for rest
this was
our private time
quiet moments
by design
the beauty of
this feelings best
i take with me
as I rest
working daily
trying to please
i admire

Entice 2

how she pleased
the vision of views
i can remember
how she was
used
and
abused
how we first met!!!!!!
she walks within
my head
always does
her plays
with mental twists
as i look on
i am confused
she sez she loves
but does she really
?
it could be said
that we are we
the rest
the adventure
for me to see:
AR

BREATH TAKEN:AR

It wasn't
the view
or the eyes
romantic thoughts
passings of mind
it wasn't
the long leg
stroked glides
the makings
of desire
a smile did touch
that a most blush
the look away
the chills
of being caught
as you steered
it wasn't
the sex play games
visions of quest
wrapPed in sheets
dimly lit
as touched
in a photo
viewed by
scented dreams
toggled
and reinforced
admirations
of
fancy
flights
dreams of
wanting
holding

Entice 2

touching
taste
stings
head bang
punches
blows to the brow
creates
those first words
that will flow
from your mouth
as she moves
past you
both do glimpse
shaded taunts
in
its flirtations
that looking down
as per the shoes
wanting to tie the nots
on your
slip on shoes
grabbing pens
looking for paper
get that number
but how will you apply
credentials in mind
relaxed is your attempt
Don't want to shatter
Don't want to scatter
your emotions peak
you begin to speak
and stumble
she has you
shaken
and torn
just what did
you want to say?

Entice 2

how will
you put it
or does your actions
explain it all

the things
you will do
to become
the noticed!!!!!
and beaten
will it be
the movement
of your dances
or the way
you take
such chances
or that
your ride
the watch
your wearing
or the jokes
you made
or will you hide?
that get to know
this targeted wine
sweetened
in its taste
of your mind
or this
your political views
miss understood
spoken wildly
just to be heard
grabbing trees
flowered laments
cries of pain
non relents

Entice 2

and in her beauty
well defined
the rose
in her steps
as she greets all
then moves by
her
silkened voice
tones
tuned your
imaginations
so siren
without
limitations
wanted lips
kisses of bliss
the dotted line
and then
the hips
nope it wasn't
that at all
but i am lying :
AR

A TAD OF POETRY WITH THE MEAL
EROTIC IT IS:AR/SH

Deep in!!!!!
the deeper
darker places
Do you roam
as the waves travel
over to

TOP
BLINDLY HUNGRY
SEEKING THAT ITCH WHICH
ALMOST
CANNOT BE FOUND
EVER SEARCHING
FOR THE PROPER FIT
HIDDEN THOUGHTS
PASS THE MIND
A NEW ROUTE
A NEW ADVENTURE
PASSION PLAYS
WITH NO BACK DROP
SIMMERED RANTS
UPON ITS PLEASURES

A fit to fix
the swerving itch
AS WE THEATER
WITHIN OUR GLIDE
CLOSING EYES
TO SEE THE TENDER
THE TAP OF MIND
TO FILL OUR PRIDES
Exquisite travel
Bent on hittinG

Entice 2

that THERE post
Still the hunger is suspended
THRILL OF Till it's flow HAS stopped
the burning IS desire S find
LOST IN LUST TILL it's endingS
Heavy breather
MOANS AND GROWNS
TWISTED FEVER
SELF INFLICTED

Show me
OF THAT your moves
INTENDED QUIPS
OR THAT OF GIST
EXPANDED PLOYS
TO PLAY WITH TOYS
ALL IN ALL
A TASTE OF FLAVOR
ONE TO SAVOR
AND ENDURE
TOUCHING IS
THE AS YOU TREMBLE
SHIVERS RUN
ALL THROUGH THE BODY
AS LAY YOU
WAITING IN STATE
ACQUIRED TASTES
A CAN RELATE
I PINCH UPON
AND KISS A NECK
A SWIRLING THOUGHT
UPON THE BREAST
A WANTED DINE
AND THEN DIVIDE
IN PLAYGROUNDS POOL
CAN YOU SWIM?:
AR/SH

JUST ON TIME

:AR/SH

As lovers
chant
RELAXED
to play
and stay
songs we meet
tis the greet
a wish
to hear
beside
the
lust
the one
that's
there
tones in flow
notes from home
Send
me a new song
One that hasn't been sung
Climb me a rainbow
Rung by rung
Run with me
in the street
of remembrance
Lest
we forget
how to have fun
I will never forget
to Have the fun
It's
a small
and just

Entice 2

a
little rhyme
just
in time
a little chime
send me
a love note
a tune
i want to hear
the gist
of a musical bliss
the ones
your heart will share
the mist inside
a musical chair
bang out songs
romantic tones
even and ever
even by phone
pls
send it please
finger taps
the table drum
kalimba
hits
even by tones
the song of words
your mind
does share
to glow the flow
ur flow
of thoughts
My heart does hunger!!!!!!!
fluid hits
past the touch
of finger tips
those burning flicks

Entice 2

the swinging hips
of wetted lips
the sweep
into turns
that flex in grind
a dance of fine
that lovers do
the gyrate
dance
all inside
its moments
chance
ALLOW ME THIS
i want to hear
the tone of you
past
emotions
body's
home:
AR/SH

MAIN EVENT:AR

IN ITS QUIET
AS YOU STEER
IN A HALLWAY
NOTHING THERE
SITTING HERE

all in
its glance
a trance
of
delights
and
fantasy
my mind spins
i see the wings
of my thoughts
how sound
it is
i
don't
know
the a door
slides open
and
she walks in
enters this hallway
and all stops!!!
a lace of grace
as grinding she
in her strides
bring
lengthy
long legged
movements

Entice 2

flow
in this motion
as she glows
to stroke
my thoughts
such rounded breasts
spoke to me
called my name
for me to see
and in its view
her body spoke
in her
structure
like
toke
of
smoke
as i viewed
her body lines
so divine
INTERESTING
and
i
rode
her
curves
as
my
mind
played
THOSE
LONG
LEGS
I've got that nerve!!!!!!
with arms extended
she move towards me
her hands out

Entice 2

oh what a thrill
my fantasy
was met
and as she touched
and as she greeted
she spoke to me
as in a song

**HI, MY NAME IS DEATH
TIME FOR US
TO MAKE LOVE
AND PLAY
ALONG !!!!! :
AR**

AS YOU LAY NEXT TO ME:AR/DH

As you lay next to me
i see the visions
the day we first made
the lovers touch
we shared
i spent time thinking
about our stream
about our steam
about our heat
about hour us
i spent time thinking
about our mist
the list
of our fantasies
i felt warmth
i felt heat
i felt your meat
in taste i allured
acquired by design
that refined you
imagined best
by your virtue
i painted this my picture
the one of anti trust
i saw the visions
within my mind
the ones of others lust
jealousy became my name
un-witted fears
of my own guilty
photos prance
upon my mind
past
that of my

Entice 2

related history
past was my mystery
past
was my miss
of worrynesses
those many many messes
those loves so lost
in my passing
my thoughts
they do wander
this woman
that I'm under
on top of me
when i shudder
and weaken
she lays
me flat
almost like
a busted cap
spent and withered
mind is splintered
wondering if
i did please her
i work hard
and sweat
tying to
give the very best
pound ruff
with no rest
till the moans
tells i beat em
then dancing
under a moon
singing bods
guess in tune?
like clair dah loone
i be pounding

Entice 2

this
my chested best
don't even want to rest
nothing can be less\
succulent
left to uncover
the radiance
of scent
rooms full
fraygered
tasted of best
pounded
rested
the close of eyes
just to remember
time left
pondering
wondering
questions of the lovers
we spent the time
pleased our minds
face the views
of our ventures

THEN REALITY SETS IN!!!!
I AM IN FEAR
I RAN MY GEARS
I AM AFRAID
I JUST GOT LAID
IS IT ME HE THINKS
WITH JUST THAT WINK
WITH JUST THAT BLINK
IS IT ME
SHE'S THINKING OF:
AR/DH

SHE WALKS WHILE SLEEPING:
AR/Connie M

INTO HER DREAMS

she glides right through
ever in coughs
her new dilemma
nights every day thoughts
she took to bed
the grandest party
inside her head
her thoughts of glory
all in a dream
her flight
in life
is her fight
dancing
upon
the prancing
across the wet ponds
of her desires
clarity in visions
that's her mission
as she seeks
the understandings
of
her traditions
in her mind
she wonders why
the things of beauty
shine her light
makes her cry
in wonder ment
just in a word
has much meanings

Entice 2

a frequent bow
in its translations
for as she sleeps
it generates
into the new day
how she reacts
decides to start a fresh:
AR/CM

IF ASKED pt 1:AR

If asked
i would
thought
you understood
given the task
if asked
i should
play with
my dreamed fantasy
the things my head sez
the very way i saw it
turning that fan past real
if thought
put into actions
that passionate play
with the deleted scenes
for doubt now on display
nothing
questionable
no cause
but much effect
in its touch
you will feel
the steam
as i blow smooth mists
of warm air
down our neck
past your ear
collected
as your shoulder buckles
as you lean back for more
as your eyes shudder
and finally close
remembering

Entice 2

how long
since the last time
did we do this
how distant is past
when presents presents
its
the time you take
to feel this as
i raise upon the other ear
taking time slowly
as your mind waits
in anticipation
to feel the joy
if asked
i move
slower still
touching hands
remove the trembles
as goose bumps rise
and you quivers
breathing heavy
gasping for
the touches of lips
as we move closer
heated is
that moment when
i touch your breast
as slowly i shower
your neck with kisses
riding up
upon your mountains
must take
that cold drink first
for you to feel
chilled lips
upon the nipples
as care and rested

Entice 2

as i lay my hand
upon your back
to lay you down :
AR

To be continued

IF ASKED 2:AR

JUST GOT TO

fell so softly ur body wakes
as I eat and lick u down,
trembles as u shake
and bend to give the suck
what the mind thinks
the body does
as reality states,
make no mistake
that fast advance
the pleasure quest
is in ur dome
go for it
let me scratch it
run my hands
then trash it
ur spirits rise
that all time high
wet events
cant relent
got to go
and get u some
NOT A WISH
AND UR SAYING U WILL DO?
WHAT DO U SAY
WHAT WILL U AGREE TO
REALITY IS NOT DISPUTED
I see u liked this one
always wanting more
lets do
and snooze
and do again
LEAST FOUR ROUNDS
FOR I WILL DROP : **AR**

IF ASKED 3:SH/AR

Under the covers
where it's warm
we have a party
for two
Sleep
is a distant thought
as play time begins
Peeling away
the things that distract
Blazing a trail of fire
leaving no blisters
only heat and passion
heat to go
this sleepless night
is its recourse
Silk, lace,cocktails
The smell of leather
and us
in fevered pitch
tethered and twisted in rhyme
Lost in this
searing heat
Desires to meet
we burn passions path
ignited and flowing
Heating up
with every move
lanterns
in the moonlight
lets give
this lust a try
it seems
to be able
to bring the extra spice

Entice 2

needed to make it sing
PEPPERED SEASON!!!!
i cringe
thoughts brought
sold and purchased
as i twist and churn
our bodies
we roast and sweat
release emotions
shoulders locked
in grand embrace
as we play
and do our fondles
as we taste
the want for more
all this
and more
well desired
only just
a praise away
pleasing you
is my desire
ONLY FOR THE ASKING!!!!!!:
SH/AR

THE BREATH OF SEX:AR/BDSP

DEEP ENTRANCE
SWEET IN DEPTH
AS I STROKE
AND RECEIVE THE RIDE
OF UR STROKES

HEIGHTENED AS
UR FEVER RISES
U SCREAM
AS I TOUCH
EACH STRIKE
DEEPER
AS I PENETRATE
AND SEARCH

SECOND WAVE
U CUM
I EAT
U SHIVER
AND MOAN

AT THAT POINT
ONLY THEN I ENTER
FEELING EACH PASS
AS U FEATHER ME
NOW WE HAVE STARTED

I STRETCH
IN HEAT
THE WHIP
OF HIPS
PASSION

Entice 2

SERGES
THE MOTIONS PEAK
THAT SWIRL
UN LIMITED
IN ITS THRUSTS

YOUR TWISTS
UNDEFINED

EACH MOVEMENT
IN TUNE

THIS CONVERSATION
IN TONGUES
AS GROOVED
LET LOOSE
AS WE SWEAT
IN OUR EMOTIONS

NOW BRING IT

Very interesting

AS I SAVOR
AND WIPE OF BROW

Give me a min.. breathing treatments

THAT'S FOR SURE
WANTING MUCH MORE

THE RUNNING GASP
AS I GRASP
AND DID CLASP

FOR THE BLOWS
YOU THROW

Entice 2

I DIDN'T KNOW
YOU SERVED!!!

BEEP BEEP BEEP BEEP

SHIT!!! FREAKING ALARM CLOCK

TIME TO WAKE UP :
AR/BDSP

HER SCENT:AR/BDSP

As quiet as
a moments notice
she arrived
within my thoughts
ever fragrant
with her eyes
so bold this
its her passion
as she rests
upon my soul
within this heart beat
is a woman giving
always with
inside her touch
bouncing always
upon her smile
the essence of
the so revealing
as she saw the paint
of this my lust
within my mind
she saw me coming
miles away as
when i ran
then up on her
she did
drop me
with that only
of her glance
hooked and tethered
like those of fish
reeled me in
as she savored
knowing had me

Entice 2

i was lost
i seem to be
that of her flavor
Her sent is in
the air just breath
as con and sold
her reverence
its tempered glass
built on the sand
with minor glare
the one she shares
shows and molds
the tint in her
for your enjoyment
now on display
i shade this day
upon my pleasant
Speechless is
the word id say
as he feeds
most inner desires
her sent becomes
stronger still
running faster even
all over his body
close ur eyes
you can see her
built in deep
upon your mind
signs of lost
ever beating
upon the chest
of want creeping
ur desires
a sip of wine
within her heart
as you are grasping

Entice 2

in night she came
warm and throbbing
ever beating
on my desire
panting heavy
as i pleased her
home of which
was my inspire:
AR/BDSP

HALIPINIO SAUCE:AR

AS IF FIRE WASN'T ENOUGH

gingerly tasted
heat past its own
slowly consumed
pouncing after dark

as i ponder
her lines glow
an education
of her body
boy i want to grow

tips of breast erect
as my tongue flows

wagging

from left to right
the ups and downs
in its flavors
as i roast
and toast
this maiden
as she seems
to hold me dear

Latin
in grace

her Spanish twirl
oh!!
she has me
and has diced me

Entice 2

almost riced me
added beans and
kinda fried me
within her warmth

the shape of lust

so inviting
most exciting
kinda blinding
all that winding
as she krumps

insights best
cant say the rest
so undressed
that her stress
she is blessed
she released
in my thoughts

zumba treats
so unleashed
as she reeled
made me wonder

shift of hips
twists and shit
bit my lip
had to grip
my venue

she then
slowed down
laid upon me
took me in
then she pound me

Entice 2

Un-even strokes
quietly gestured
with a shift
couldn't just guess
her movements best
threw me off
within her timing
took my brain
right off my rhyming

seat-belts on
enjoyed the ride
oh this glide
so enticing

hard it seems
to articulate
this my state
at this rate
when she rose up

she came down
with a hit
bit my lip
a second time

as i trembled
wanting more
hit the floor
of my basement

ihh this meal
cant conceal
but it is real
within her passion

Entice 2

as she stroke
and had me toke
and lit me up
that's no joke

serious ass
this our bash
can bank that cash
continue ass

love commands
lust demands
make some plans IE
got to have it

that note
from home
or one on phone
exotics best
erotic tests
just cant rest
just like the pepper

i must follow

and in it all
and as it stands
those great demands
away from home
notta mass
poor some more
or poor favor
i k and lindo
i learned spanish :
AR

WHAT'S HIDDEN UNDERNEATH:SH/AR

I PAINTED YOU A PICTURE
ONE FOR YOU TO SEE
ARE YOU REALLY SURE
YOU SEE ME

So you think YOU SAY you know me
have you looked WELL deep within
what do you see
when the door is open
then it just begins

my mind has many things in it
many thoughts
are going through

when you think
you know

some things that seem

is often

WHEN

At the back
of my mind

THAT IS WHERE
YOU WILL START

will you be careful

and take a look

Entice 2

in and
not behind

tell me what you see

would you
like to hear

thoughts THAT
i will share

trying to be
IF so kind
LOOK INSIDE
YOU WILL FIND

my heart
has
some scars

DENTS THERE TOO

AS IF U KNEW

if you see them

please take care

you may never know
who, what

has put them there

maybe

for me to grow

Entice 2

perhaps for me

to REALLY shine

my life has taken

many twists + turns

this you could

and would say

I'm in my movie
SHOWING EACH DAY

of my life

seems

on display

So you say

you think you know me

just be still

and you will see

to that

what

do you think

how do you KNOW

Entice 2

just don't see

GROW AND LEARN

you have to feel

me with your heart

THE REAL IN ME

you should know

the things I'VE DONE

THINGS OF WHICH

that's in my mind

ok now

how do you see

that of my heartS

SHOWN GROWN picture

has some scars

and bumps THERE TOO

that i
must repeat

if you see them

please take some care

Entice 2

you may never know

who+what

has put them there!!!!!

a lesson plan

with much despair

you have to feel

The me in me

the me within
all your heart

and know THIS

in THE mind you see!!!!!!

this is

just the start

so you say

I'm what you want

are you sure

you can start

this relationship
of the minds

Entice 2

so you say
I'm what you need
can you conceive
to that my feels

built by time
in my rhyme
my quest is

I aim to please

·we are not

so miles apart

don't you run

stick around

lets have some fun

if you

take the time

really read

my insides

wills:
SH /AR

THAT NIGHT:

BILLIE DEE SMITH PIRELA/AR

This evening
dark and cold
as we lay
by an open fire
sharing a blanket
he cradles her
as a warm glove
as he strokes her softly
you can hear him say
come here my sweet
I've been reading your soul
for sometime now
don't try and run
from it anymore
i promise you
i wouldn't
feed your soul
with anymore pain
allowed
is to feed your soul
the passion
you've been in need of..
now please
my sweet love
stop fighting!!!
come here
my sweet love
I've been reading your mind
for sometime now
don't run from it
anymore
I've been reading your body lang
and i see that you've never

Entice 2

had someone reach
your inner side
that one
that is in need
of a strong soul
to feed
shhhh !!!
don't talk my sweet
let me show you
how this goes
what this talking is about..
as he lays her
on a soft bed of roses
he starts
to talk
to her
with each touch
as he communicates
the body motion
she can't fight him!!!
any longer
as he starts to kiss
inches of her body fine..
the sigh and slight moan
with every stroke
like roasted rubs
within this heat
her body
a mystic playground.
his desire
the drive\
of which
he knows the road
as they continue
light kisses
to the eyelids
peak

Entice 2

a slight blow
upon the ears
she begins to tremble
to open the blouse
so he may fondle

HE CAN READ
HER DESIRES
IN HER
SOFT GREEN EYES
HE IS MORE THEN WILLING
TO SATISFY EACH ONE OF THEM
HE is BEGGING
TO SOFTLY LICK
HE HEARS THE MOANING
DOESN'T EVEN THINK
FOR A MINUTE
\OF HIS SEXUAL NEEDS
HE IS ENJOYING THE TASTE
OF HER SWEET JUICES
HE MOVES EVER SO slowly
DOWN HER BODY
SHE STARTS TO FEEL
HER PELVIC MUSCLES NEEDING
THE PURE ECSTASY
HAS HER SCREAMING
HIS NAME IS OUT
HIS KISS
HER SOFT BREAST CALLS
SHE STARTS TO FEEL
HER INNER WARMTH
GROWING STRONGER
HE CAN HEAR
HER SOFT SEXY VOICE BEGGING
HIM NOT TO STOP
HE KEEPS HIS LIPS
KISSING EVERY INCH OF HER

Entice 2

MAKING SURE HE BREATHS
AND SAVORS
ALL OF HER
INTO HIM HE KNOWS
THAT HE IS GETTING READY
TO BRING TO HER
A NIGHT OF HOT PASSION

THAT NIGHT :AR/BDSP

SHE WEPT:AR

like those of raindrops
as she cried
romances blisses of sex
as she released
and in that she wept
with her inner fears withheld

so long she held her emotions
refused the release
of her heart
in different times

younger best
ohh so so loose
her release
uncontrolled

as age set in
it took the gin
to rave edge that
her insecurities

looseness of wine
or that of kind
mamas teachings
so un yielding
so restrictive
of this device

broke that door down
then broke her heart
cause he wont stay
to pave her way

Entice 2

bitter walls
are those in front
felt the fall
as i went in

the pinch

the quest
upon her neck
rub of the breast
brokered a sweat
ohh shes warm now !!!!

then the shift
the hands placed
upon the waist
of her long beauty

think of fruit
the ones u taste
the sweetness is
in the first bite

eyes so closed
as u nibble
then comes the juice
of the first bite
ohh such nice
do you follow

ummm the sweetness
of this taste
the thought of sugar
can u relate

loss of control

Entice 2

in her whimper
the drawbridge fell
as she limbered
as lights got dimmer

her virgin thoughts

bashed by trance
man with lance
that scary waltz
can u relate

she held it dear
out of fears
workin with it
quite a choir

like a drug
the first taste
like the first date
it might take time
can you fathom

now she rocks
like that of clock
and when she drops
the tears do follow hmmm???? :
AR

IN THE MOVEMENT:AR

SITTING IN THE CORNER
QUIETLY IN THE DARK

WATCHING

AS THE FOLKS WALKED IN
STILL SILENT
FOR THOSE INFANT MOMENTS
AS SHE WALKED IN
FOR THOSE OF US
IN THE PLACE
THE LOOK AND STARE
THE ONES WITH GRACE

WHO WOULD KNOW
THE SHOWS THEY BROUGHT
A COMMON SCENE
FOR THIS THAT NIGHT
AND OHH MY GOD
WAS QUITE A SIGHT

WHO WOULD HAVE THOUGHT
THE BEAMS OF LIGHT
PROJECTED HEIGHTS
OF SHOWS AND FLOWS
DRAMATIC BEST
OF ROLLS THEY PLAYED
EVENTFULL GAMES
AND MESSES MADE

WHEN IT HAPPENED
I DON'T KNOW
MUST HAVE SLIPPED ME
AT THE DOOR

Entice 2

SO NICE THE SLICE
OF HER VENUE
CONSIDER THIS
THAT SHE KNEW

ITS AT THAT GLANCE
PURE FANTASIES
I VIEWED THE CHANCE
TO GAZE AGAIN

A NON RELATED POKE OF FAITH
SEEN HER BEFORE
IN MY DREAMS

AS GRACED HER MOVEMENTS
IN MY THOUGHTS
AS SHE GLIDED PAST ME
FOR JUST THAT MOMENT

IT WAS THAT DANCED MOMENT
SHE HIT THE FLOOR
AS MUSIC WARMED UP
TO SHOW SOME MORE

THE BEAT OHH THE BEAT WAS TALKING
COULD NOT ESCAPE

AS BODIES SHUCK
AND BEGAN TO WAVER
AS HEADS DID TURN
WITH ITS GYRATE
THAT FEELING OF
GET LOOSE AND SHUDDER

SWIRLED THOSE HIPS

Entice 2

THE SPEECH OF THUNDER
DROP IT DOWN
MAKE EM RUMBLE
UR IN THE PLACE
NO DISGRACE
CLOSE YOUR EYES
AND LET UR BODY TALK
AND FEEL THE PRESSURE

COMMUNICATION IS WONDERFUL
ALL OF ITS LEVEL
BUT IN THIS PLACE
ITS PHD

MUSICS UP!!!
AND SO SHE ROSE
THAT 5.8
FROM HEAD TO TOE

AND AS SHE MOVED
TO FLOOR OF DANCE
HER BODY MOVES
UNSPOKEN TRANCE

AS SLIDES WOULD HAVE IT
IT WAS SMOOTH
HER HEAD SEEMED LIKE
IN A GROOVE
BODY LANG
ON THE MOVE
THE TWIST
THE MOTIONS
ALL EMOTIONS

FREEDOM OF TODAY'S EVENTS!!!

Entice 2

FREEDOM OF RELATIONSHIPS RENT!!!

FREEDOM TO EXPRESS UR PLIGHT!!!

FREEDOM UR BEHINDS IN FLIGHT!!!

FREEDOM ITS FRIDAY NIGHT!!!!

NOW AND FOREVER

BACK TO THE DANCE

THE BASS FLAGGED A FUNKY NOTE
THE BOTTOM OF WHICH
HIT THAT LOW SUB TONE

THE HIGH HATS SPOKE
TINGLES UNKNOWN
GROUND ON HOME
THE FUNKY

LEAD GUITAR SANG
TO BRING THIS DRAMA CLEAR
TO SHATTER ONES MIXED EMOTIONS
THE STAGE PLACE IS HERE
THE DANCE FLOOR

AND THAT DRUM
A KICKING TAP
BASS DRUM HIT
ON THE BOTTOM
FLOORED THE FLOW
MADE ME TREMBLE
STOOD RIGHT OUT
IN THE RUMBLE

Entice 2

AND IN THE BACK A BANJO PLAYED
REMEMBRANCES OF PAST EVENTS
THE CULTURE SHOCK
 OF FUNKY DUDES
ALL OF THIS
WELL IN TUNE

AND AS SHE DANCED
HER ROCKIN SHAKES
MADE ME STOP
AND SIT AND WONDER
COULD IT BE
MY FANTASY
BUT SEE IN ME
AS FEVER ROSE HIGHER
AS SHE MOVED THAT LEG
AND SHOOK HER BODY

I JUST WANT A TASTE!!!!!!:
AR'
December 8, 2013
the quiet creative space
Like ·
Seen by 6
Connie Moretz likes this.
Kim Morrow
Write a comment...

'IN THE BASEMENT

A WELL OF DEPTH:AR

i sit hear
in this basement
alone and with my thoughts
so dark is this room
surrounded by the lonely
the fate that i established
reasons based upon my ego
the place of dummy's fair
neglect of seeing reality
not knowing the truth of love

How deep is this feeling
the path i took for us
how far away this reach
the proper mustn't touch it
how weakened i still feel
how blinded by dirty slaps

i miss that of your body tone
the music and the   cords
the themes of streams
of the love well missed
the un rehearsed reflex

our witted responses
we did make
right in tune
rhymes in flux
and on the note

I miss the tender kisses

Entice 2

the bass in the baritone
how scented was this feel
painted visions
in its taste
the warmth of a feeling
possessed by touch

to desire the contact
of this hearts mate
to blend this drunk of wines
to savor each given moment
the fill of your divine

beat me still
yes it does
i cant feel
others of others
i find it hard
to find the fever
I'm lost by thought
in ur tenderances
I'm in a hate
of my mistaken-ed
rejected thoughts
i am un grate
full of self
without reason
best mist
its the season

a fear that
happens when
hearts unsettled

remembering then
those times a and reasons

Entice 2

THE REAL IS THIS!!!!!!

IN YOUR TOUCHES

My life is going
i must be true
as i miss you
the things i did not say!!!!

ur presents
more than Christmas
as brilliant as snows with the wise love given

how sensual and ohh so real
as fingers   pinched my soul
as i entered you
with your eyes open
you saw my heart
and my weakened body
as i wilted in your arms
make ring those
the blessed hours
the home i knew
and wanted

comforts best
i found no other
so pure its face
as mirrors shine

reflecting us
as we made love
our personal show
to give more drive

the fears of loosing you
to others desires

Entice 2

i think my
jealous ways
the roads taken
pushed you away
if I'm not mistaken

Its been five years
since you left
i sit and wait
for the return
as in a bird
or so it goes

this basement deep
the thoughts are deeper
a well of souls

i didn't   mean
  to kill her lover
i was confused
i thought there was no other
so -------- :
AR'

REMEMBER THE BLANKET

Extended:

AR/Giimerci Rodriguez/Ed Coonce

Remember that blanket?
the one that ment secure,
remember how great it felt,
the texture so serene ,
remember when the way the day went ,
you could curl up and rest ur head ,
for this u didn't pay rent.
cause you know things went bad.

The re in members played a part,
the gates we all ran through,
friends played away the troubles of your mind,
the over your head flew ,
bad events,
bruised knees
,weaken heals
bandaged by tears
of fears,
mom,
the love of your life
she was always there .

Now time has past ,
it was a blast,
the mom we knew
turned into mom/babe
Babe baby ,
tough love women,
you be

Entice 2

my blanket now.

I enter you
and probe ur mind ,
ur body is my adventure
you hold the keys
to my locker,
the cabinet
that hides my blanket..

your heart is home to me,
the campfire
mash mellow burning ,
eye candy view sharing,
rejection giving
sweated brow equity reaching
hider of my blanket.
cant you
come out and play?
the holder of my blanket.

please don't
take my fun away

Other days
come and go ,
today i feel
your needs
i hope that
as i fill that grief
we play
up under that blanket

That silence of lamadrugada peace
fill your blankets
covering your
restless emotions

Entice 2

and the dew of dawn ,
you wake up
in each cell,
celebrating a new day,

A hair can split sunlight
and cast a shadow
for only a moment
In that brief time

in that thin blade
of darkness
all the hopelessness
and hubris in this earth
hides
good night :
AR /Ed Coonce'/GM

IT'S TIME:AR

W e have come to a moment
this moment in time
this thing between us
discourses in our rimes
lovers new renditions
tunes played
once and again

the well beaten drum
double time
in its beat
the curse
of kindred harmonies
trenched in our souls

so weathered
this drum is
whipped on by time

how deep
of the bass
kick stomp
as the rhyme theme flows

the things
we have often said
this period well defined
the period with endings
we blessed
the start of something new

spoken were
the words did pass
alas the new thought flew

Entice 2

from this
the constant interact
almost as if we knew

the shelf
we placed our selves upon
as trinkets
they did share

placement
and crowds did dance
in this position

past the fears
they were there
to pat the back of fools
Mr and Mrs understood

how blind this stumble
may have been
it was the grin
that saved us all

it was that of gestures
the polish shined
  on throws
of our diplomat
the lengths
  of which we grew

tis to be said
the talk of hearts
the trusts rebuilt
those home grown facts
the no relax
tears alibi

Entice 2

wept and slept
made love till dawn
and so we crept
loss is not an option

So this time we have
to land the prize
to feel whats real
reject demise
to face a fear
stepping across
in gods hands
he holds all thoughts

the time has come
for you to make your trip
i feel the lonely
this too is real
ill sit and wait
for your return
ill hope the best
in you i trust :
AR'

RIVER BANKS:AR

THERE!!!!

By the edge
of the water
views of passer bys
sucking up
the sun of the lover
tanned by desire

a daze and viewed
your stroll by
drove to home
the want

every given step
a mind sweep
as your lines flow

so graced
is your movement
a stride to forever
t hat want on desire
the visual paint
of you en graced

my distant view
not so far
away from you
but fixed and focused
a daze
i cant pass
imagination filled
behold the still
photo engraved

Entice 2

is it so?
the glow you render
defender
for beauty sake
no mistake
I'm hooked

i wish
you would feel
the need
ur still
presents
clears the guess
of who u are

i have to know you
i want to show you
of my intent
hope to glow you
just lay there

i know your river
and how it flows
i sit on the banks
as i watch

i want to swim
in your tide
i want to glide
inside your wave

can you just know me
and tend to show me
past relevant
of those that left

i want your heat

Entice 2

past penetrate
the flow of thought
make no mistake

please speak to me
i want your tone
can you phone
for me to answer:
AR

BREATHING HEAVY:AR

Wasn't it
so long ago
then remembered
this our show

as stepping out
all in our party
those friends around
wasn't it hearty

the drinking glass
we used to share
now its empty
your not there

quiet nights
ohh so cold
could not replace
the your so bold

speeches of songs
gone and missed
the touches of warmth
in the mist

Did i
leave all this
just to learn
my answered quest
it fell apart

a written in stone
the love was solid
now that we are grown

Entice 2

and all departed

blemished sweet kisses
now reminisces
tainted lust
that of paints
on the wall
of my heart

the room i run to
in my mind
to fill the feel
left behind

thin is
my resolved
the fallen victorious
of my stupidities
somehow learned
infidelities

i weep inside
i miss the rides
i now despise
what should have been:
AR

SHE DROPPED IT:

BILLIE DEE SMITH PIRELA/AR

BEEN DOING THIS FOR WEEKS
working hard each day
sometimes without pay
he knew how past a beauty mark
she was
the eyes
the body
the legs
and breast
now wow!!!!
hips
with that sexy dip
the gracious smile
dimpled and dreamy
little girl charms
that way she walked
the sight a harm
painful at best
he wondered why
the love she gave him
one would almost cry

DID SHE LOVE HIM
HMM I WONDER

he was weak
bin on his feet
nothing
to show for
his hard labor
time to close
this he knows
don't want to go home

Entice 2

he is ashamed!!!!!!
wants to run and hide
there went his pride
wished he would die
so from there he made a call
said that he would be home late
a drink he had to take
seemed to make the thing
seem better
his inter hesitate!!!!
aww but if he only knew
the things that she saw through
the weekend just began
lovin was the plan
of wHich he was a fan
but now he is crushed!!!!!!
seems she already knew
the glass she saw thru
and when she answered the call
and in her comments
pinned him on the wall
said she:!!!!!!
you asked of me to bring u out
to meet your sexual desires
and in that I set this plan
to get u even higher
I've been hoping to lay
you on my bed
ready to show your body
everything your mind
has been feeding for..
his mind begins to wonder!!!!!!!
stay there don't speak
I will take care of you..
let her be your deepest motivation!!!!!!
this ran through his mind
of this mountain

Entice 2

he can climb
now you mind blow
the mind of
this simple man
yes ill go there !!!!!
.feeding him is what makes her wet
in his mind
its then ill start after rest and do my own
ill sweat weakened
and in the excitement drool for i want more
of ur twists and turns as u slowly stroke
that hip with delivery of hormone blows
and at its peak,
as i try to control and recover
u hammer me
breath heavy in the thought
breathing heavy dark after
gasping for air
making each of your fantasy's become her deepest desires
to fill
with hot sweet passion
.he is thinking!!!!!!!!!!
just to watch as u quiver
and shake the heat
of ur trembles
as u frantically flex
and the bed
walks across the room
,my mind at that point !!!!!!!!!
is to see if i can get u to faint
in ur passions,as i apply
to the women you've slept with
in many ways
feeding off her
like she was your last meal
the mind persuaded!!!!!!!!!!!!
he ran home

Entice 2

breaking land speed records
his lust lasted
3 days
she nick named him after !!!!!!
and put it in the news paper
in the last columns
under
OBITUARIES!!!!!!!!!!!!!!!!!:
AR/BDPS

Entice 2

SHE HOLDS HER OWN:AR

Always knowing
she has to stand
moments lonely
the grace of tan
the crowd
of the quiet room
into her thoughts
life does loom
the dreams of
Mr Right
a school girls gist
past is of this time
a flick of the wrist
SHE
stands
looking
at her realities
always knowing
the path
she streaks
always finding
the roads
well taken
how then is it
for sight
is it
her gift to share
how is it then
alone at home
the many
of
no one's there
she
c
of painted glass

Entice 2

alas
standing
romancing
dancing
prancing
with lights
an artistry
drawn dim
her cares
drawn
on backboard sheets
all to grow
in the show
of i don't know
the black board
sketch
inside her eyes
the despise
of
her past of life
former wives
of shredded tears
we see the many
with their fears
broken
beaten
cheated on
left upon
as they grind
their way of life

SHE KNOWS
the root
of the truth
a dance
of the knowledge
that she lived thru

Entice 2

SHE KNOWS
herself instead
the things
well dread
and the dead
of her plight
the past of lovers
their paths now gone
curbed and sided
with no look back

SHE KNOWS
her change of mind
and how it shifts
past the inches
now just a flick
echh sez sive
comp pulsed sive
the twist of fate
a non and relate
able!!!!!!
tarnished blows
met her toes
and in all that

SHE HOLDS HER OWN
NOW
she paints herself
the electric fence
with the tape
and the
insulation
of
herself
:AR

JUST A STIFF VACATION

ALL THE REASONS TO CONJURE
BROKEN PT 2:AR

What exactly
was she thinking
all the reasons
to grin and wink
unhappy
within her missing
from the foutain
a use for drinking
justifications
a word
so wide in link
reasons for
a taste of drink
a wine refreshed
with every glass
past that door
and touch of class
ohh yes
the years gone by
ohh yes
a heart does fry
but
to find the reason
for the treason
one must conjure
that find to play
the things held
to state the fate
just to find
a way to lay
HER PRESENT LOVER!!!
A fairly good man

Entice 2

indeed!!!!!!
wasn't really
a taste that
she needed
but a seem
to be stable
in all she heeded
inside her heart
the flavor stood
sometimes kicking
sometimes missed
and understood
that cry for flavor
inside a touch
that body of sweat
the one that savors
the strokes of hand
across the body
to penetrate
the lust
also well hidden
she shares
with many tears
the warmth of chills
when the
real he is near
she hears his tone
outside his moans
as they sliver
in
romances touch
she feels
his tender
inside his trembles
as she awakens
the song of lust
she raises

Entice 2

her hopes
ahh !!!!!
hes the same
and of his lovin
her great escape
that nay of gates
that clouds the other!!!!!
but now
to justify
a reason to tell
that gray test
of lie
to shrug
the fates
is her mistake
as his fever
then relates
she saw his truth
inside his leaving
knowing better
of her self
but ohh
his touch
his body rush
his to handle
without the fuss
inside his fervor
the lights go OUT
the truth did speak
it spoke to her
but the message
not there to hear
FLAVOR SPOKE!!!!!
its loudest words
that she heard
it called her name
NOW ONLY

Entice 2

TO JUSTIFY !!!!!!!!
forgetting the hearts
always broken
forget all bets
WHATS IN A LIE ???????
TRUTHS ARE TOLD
BUT ARE THEY REALLY??????
VOICES HEARD
BUT ARE THEY SPEAKING?????
VISIONS SEEN
INSIDE THE HEAD
IT STAYS WITH US
UNTIL WE R DEAD
the truth here is
her lover is loved
but
the one that left
HE IS THE ONE!!!!!!!
open and on
is his return
what would you do?
IF THIS IS
ALL YOU HEARD
:AR

BROKEN PT 1

**SHE SITS
IN WAITING
DREAMING
OF TIMES PAST
WONDERING IF HE
IS THE SAME**:AR

Time has not
been
the best of friends
for her or him
his touch
so long ago
so longed for
he now
has returned
to her home
and has made the call
upon his arrival
(note then)
he still lives
his journey
to far off lands
has brought back
his return
to find himself
is what he said
to leave behind
his confusion
to build upon
a nest of eggs
to gain the cash
of his missions
a part of his
delusion

Entice 2

to be the man
self told to be
to sail upon
his tranquil sea
but in his mind
he fared her so
and some of time
he wished
to let her go

HER BEAUTY SCARED HIM
in first her glance
never knowing
if
he had a chance
his cares were weak
in all
he glanced
for in her eyes
she seemed
a trance
and so he ran
to far a way
never thinking
of this day
shadowed past
had his ass
and as he danced
he saw her face
every touch
of another
his mind was sent
to his lover
every kiss
his lips did taste
could not remove her
from his gaze

Entice 2

in as for
the body's rubbed
the brain would speak
about the tugs
he remembers
her silkened touch
he remembered
her slow to rub
he sought after
a new of lines
to replace
her body fine
structured lengths
her body showed
legs of strength
as they glowed
wrapped in silk
the sheets did bear
of the lust
she did share
as she rose
to service him
the sleek and slender
saw his grin
so smooth her stroke
turn on the fans
to cool the beast
she had at hand
as they churned
inside the moans
his hands did pat
her body tones
the mirrored image
with eyes wide closed
to see the savor
as she rose
oh !!!!!

Entice 2

did she quake him
a taste refined
inside this glass
her body's wine

REPEATEDLY!!!!!!~
THE NIGHTS ADVANCE
the scary thought
that he was broken
the non of stop
could not replace
a love well shared
so far in grace
again and then
the gaze of lace
inside his mind
he never knew
as hours flew by
and hunger spoke

MORNING CAME
inside a frown
last nights events
now on the ground
as he did think
was one night only
might not be able
to show her boldly
and so he ran
so far away
only the return
was made this day
he would
find his way
and return
to her some day

Entice 2

LOVE NEVER LEAVES
IT ALWAYS SPEAKS
TO THOSE OF US
OUTSIDE THE SHEETS
HOW DID SHE FEEL????????:
AR
                    BROKEN PT1

THE

BROKEN

STORY

CAN THIS BE FIXED???

Entice 2

This is a tale of a women ,who lived and was raised in Romania. She knew and lived through communism, betrayal, dominance, and maltreatment. Now she is in America. It begins with her coming into womanhood.

She, the daughter of a farmer, at 22yrs of age, looking to her future, romance is under way. Dictated to by her father, ruled by the new husband, she was his gift, a family pledge; a given women who knew not the caring of love. As the story goes:

I was new to this world called marriage, given to dreams of what could be. My life was to learn how to please him and to give to this man I never even knew.

Many years, I stayed with him; I think 9 in all. I saw the upside down that led to his downfall. He said he would go and work, make some money he would. But when frustrated by the day, he'd go out and drink; drunk and misunderstood. He lived for the opinions of other's desire, living to give mistakes requested by his friends, that I be given to them, so that they may lay. He obliged their requests and brought this thing to me. To be the obedient wife, he hoped I'd agree.

I was supposed go along with this, or so he thought. This was the custom of men in this village, a lot of women went through. This is the shit we women took to get along with them. Dictatorship begins at home, it has no throne, just avenues of disgust rule the highway of insecurities. The King created a no love zone. I'd make love to him, this was my duty. My feelings gone away; never to be found again.

I lost the feeling of touch although I never knew the feelings of me. I felt like a circumcised women without the mental blisses. I know I have my needs and how to get it done, by myself alone. There is no room for fun. The only goose bumps were from the shower.

I came to America with this in my rear view. I came here to this land and here I met you. Didn't know how to receive your love, I'm barely getting through. If time can heal, I'll let you in to feel what's real, the me inside my heart. I will begin anew... you ..have to learn. This my vents, you have to stand and pay the rents of this house I call me...

Part 2

My love for you is new to me, please understand. I find this fresh, please understand. I want to refresh this.. to begin again. I wish to show you some of my pains, please understand, it's not in vain..please understand. What I felt, the old views and the words I fought. The husband's speech:

Woman..
you do not listen to me;
obedience you do not know?
I've made you my wife,
you must listen,
you are my cattle,
like that goat in the barn,
like the cow in the field,
the horse that runs about,
You're mine for the taking,
you must fulfill my needs
yet when I bend u over, it seems you have no feels.
It's you I bought,
land and all,
You're at my whim and I gotta have it.
Your job is to please me and my friends alike,
you know how this goes.

Entice 2

I had my friends wife
just the other night..
This is our way,
You're a toss away
to feed the needs in me.
You are my shine,
I put on the table,
the statue,
I can show my friends,
You're in my stable.
You eat because of what I do,
You sleep cause of this house I built,
and like the fruit I pluck,
I eat and throw away,
on any day,
you must consent,
without relent,
and resentment.

Is this what I bought?
I follow my trend,
and in this,
I thought you were my friend. Thought you'd understand,
this lay of the land
all you women must get used to.
You have no room to be a sheep,
and eat all before,
That's at your feet
Your job is to feed the need in me,
I'm in control, the boss of this home,
I'm your friend, lover, mother, sister and brother
rolled into one.
You live because of me,
make no mistake,
there is no gate,
no road out to your road to freedom.
You decided your plight,

Entice 2

the day we were married, there is no flight..

Her vents:
We are not together on this...

Part 3

I also had my say in the matter:

To think of me as cattle says a lot about you,
within these years,
all that I've been through,
try to imagine
my point of view.
As I see it,
you got no clue.
Many many years ago, when we first met,
you showered me with gifts,
made the promise to my father,
to expand his land,
did a grand stand,
said by you.
You must marry me and build me a home,
said you would be true,
to me anyway,
but that was just a lie.
There are so many things you spoke,
given all these years,
but in these times,
these many tears,
torture and frustration,
these things I've gotten to know.
You promised me you wouldn't drink,
the stink of your clothes tells me other,

Entice 2

And how you share you with another.
Your behavior,when you're drunk,
only dogs do that instead.
You jump on me,
when we are in bed
Then beat me if i resist.
You pressure me with your friends.
our romance is totally dead.
Like the lying flowers you almost bought,
like the fake tears and a fart.
Your touch is that of pine needles brush,
a rush to please yourself.
A drunken lush, hailed in musk,
cows feces on your shoes,
you clearly stink up the place.
You hope I'm in the mood.. you try to hand me to your
friends,
thinking I'll agree.
I'm an educated woman,
this I know you see.
I have no need to be a steed and
carry someone else's seed.
All respect is gone,
found itself a new home;
the way of love, this is not.
You complain I bore you no children,
when all you shoot is blanks,
The esteem was lost,
just me being your wife;
Your carriage is just a front.
You don't know who you are.
maybe your friends can relate,
once past the gate,
that one they call a bar.

No children will I bring up on the top of this war.
It seems to me you've reach and found the end to this farce.

Entice 2

I'm leaving you with this failure,
no way shall I regret, the many times
you abused me,
the hurts have built this wall.
The many times,
I only regret knowing you at all.
How many years must I endure?
No man, you just gotta fall.
I have no need for another
if this is how it will be.
I'll comfort myself,
and bring me to my knees.
How bitter I must feel,
you won't even defend my honor.
How bitter you feel
I want no other,
not even you can press this point.
The health you dented
with this your life,
style has a name,
it ain't yours.
Redress yourself,
You'll be alone,
and with no phone..
Who will you call
now that your alone?
Who's wife shall you dethrone
to call your very own..
yet to give away..

Part 4

..there are those things
before this, I refused to tell you.
makes no difference now, the gate is open.
Remember the days you left me at home with that your uncle

Entice 2

and your son.
They thought they would have their way with me
as told by your first born.
I fought and got out of there, hid in the barn as free as you
may think.
I didn't come with this farm.
It seems you have lost your place..the big disgrace within the
realm of man if you think this is a common mistake.
I failed to do that their plan.
Couldn't turn to you, your future runs done like a broken light,
the rapist are now on the run, twas the end of their fun, (as you
may think).

It seems to me you must impress,and for this you are bested,
in another land they would be arrested.
You need a lot of help. Your views and thoughts have been
quite blind,your selfish ways cause your delays of life.
The pains I would receive,to play this game,you think me a
cow, a goat perhaps; a piece of meat that you must share.
The glooms come close to you, confusion now is your best
friend. You have destroyed my vessel of youth,
you have enslaved my young friends too.
You made me this you see, now take your pay;
I will be free.
You have gained my hatred's vest with all the rest.
I see you least.
I'm stronger now, I have no shroud.
Kept my respect, kept my family at best without the incest
planned for me.
The women you see has no greed, has now herself to feed and
can do it well.
Remember then the love you lost, remember now when we
first started, remember the warmth there used to be and in all
this remember me.
This women you see standing before you is now free from
your threats, beatings, rape and frozen heart.
The damage is minor, my life is my reward.

Go out and find another to test, go out and find one among the
rest. I truly wish you the best.
Before I die, I won't think of you; a bad memory past
entering my rear view.
I know who I am, I Havarti plan with much love to give...
lust be my companion...

Part 5

Her Vindication:

As the gods would have it, she walked out that gate, the
owner of the American's lottery (Visas) sealed the deal of her
fate. Her journey was far from his reach; 10 years had past her
by. She carried even to this day the pain's sweet minted pie.

Browsed this our country side,open was her lot and
sometimes she reviews her past, treating the elderly, for it was
safe and away, out lover's gates, until the day she met me.

Like those of us that put our love in pets we trust. Those
critters we reach out to to cover our disdain, those needy
friends we bring home and then we have our needs met; a true
someone to love. Like our dog Lucky who shivers when we
touch who barks at us when we approach; a part of us is free
and so is he, as needy as the we. Abused in his youth, she
brought him home and like she, he stays with us. I open doors
but he doesn't run. He watches us for the look of his life but
that's another story to be continued.

I listen to that her pains every day, the cause to maybe I
should run away but I stay. Firm and hardened by my lives
learned, I have the trust in us. On top of this...it's been another

10 years for us. In me she has trust but when we met if you give me away, that's the end of us.

"Please hear my pains I live everyday, they won't go away in me. I feel alone when you're not home. I reach for you, the one I touch. I call your phone to see if you will reach home, I beat your thoughts because to me you're the boss. You are the man I choose. I see that you have a love for me ,with all my faults, you must agree and kneel to my wants. You must be strong and understand me. We are miles a part, culture and history, but our tastes are the same; first and third.."

"..the world's we grew; it is the home for me and you. It is the bread I eat, it is the the meal of thoughts, the new views of my teachings. The things I see that remind me of he. Those things remembered, the things I scream at, those thoughts I try to forget. The time it takes for me to feel the lust in love, a new avenue with no road to obligation. To renew what's warm and moist is new for me so honey do let's take our time.."

"..I do love you but remember I have eaten this pain for so long, it has become the sweet meal I feel. The only thing I know to digest; it will never go away. With this you must live.. with us..me and Lucky, the three of us.."

Many a woman has had to feel these pains we create and we judge those who sometimes run away. Some of us have made dents to relieve the pain. That's our rent I pay each day for his mistakes. I love her best as she stands stellar, but just to let you know...
I wouldn't have it any other way!!!

Andre Roberts and Friends

Entice 2

In Honor of Broken Hearts Renewed by

Fantasies of the Erotic

BEFORE HER
HE STANDS
THINKING HE'S
THE BETTER MAN!!!!
FIZZLED
BY HIS THOUGHTS
INTENSITY RISES
HOT
AND PERSPIRED
THE FLARE
OF THIS ROAST
FOR HIM
SHE'S TOAST
COVERS DRAWN
AR/ALR

...Sees the desires
in his eyes
Realizes now
is the time
Even if
it's just
for tonight
Here and now
feels so right
With a heavy exhale
she bites her lip
To the floor
the gown does slip
With hungry eyes

Entice 2

she beckons him
And within seconds
against the wall
she's pinned
as fevers rise
insider her
the prize
the moisture
read
inside
his head
inside
this dream
the dream that led
no time
for
small of talk
a want
to
plant
injected
froth
pinned
and passioned
was his fashion
an aggressive grab
to launch the stab
no thought
of what
tomorrow brings
on flesh he climbs
till ears will ring
no slow in this
just grab for hips
to raise her high
then slip and
dip

Entice 2

but passions have
a funny fate
and of the time
ohh
it was late
he must
have had
too much
to drink
that fevered bliss
that all time hit
was low in show
and hit the snow
for it was over
within a blink
Dark
are the
memories
of what
had happened
in side his head
his mind was
rappin
ohh
of
that hangover
the claim of fame
the show is over
and when he woke
on the ground
the love he lusted
was not around
psst
i say
he must have been
its at this point
his ears did ring

Entice 2

while laying there
on the ground
memory lost
lost of round
wandering if
it was his play
or maybe
about this try
another day

ABOUT HER BOYFRIEND !!!
SHE NEVER TOLD HIM
ABOUT THE LUST
THAT ONE NIGHT ONLY
ABOUT HER HABIT
SHE BOUNCED LIKE RABBIT

only time will tell
inside her reign
the if and when
if luck will gain
if again the she
will want to play
and if
inside her wants
she will see him again
another day!!!

AR/ALR

About The Author

Andre Roberts is a veteran who served his country well and proudly. He is now retired and has traveled to many distant and exotic places. This helps add the flava to his unique style of writing and poetry. He constantly supports and engages other artists and has no problem allowing them to have the spotlight.

He poetry is deeply sensual yet spiritual and he often salts it with stories of foreign lands and peoples. He is a man rich in culture and richly interested in the cultures of others. His work is to be enjoyed and praised as he takes us on his journey.

He is the author of two previously released books of poetry. The heritage rich "When The Kingdom Fell" and the sensually peppered "Entice". This, his third offering, BROKEN & EROTIC, is a collection of poetry mixed with the woes of the broken hearted and lonely as well as the desires and fantasies of the erotically inclined. Nothing can cure a lonely, broken spirit like pure romance and sensuality!

Entice 2

Author/Poet Andre Roberts